In memory of Deborah Brodie,
my friend and teacher
—S.R.B.

For Mom and Dad
—K.W.

All Kinds of STRONG

by **Sharon Reiss Baker**

illustrated by **Kris Wiltse**

This **PJ BOOK** belongs to

_____

_____

JEWISH BEDTIME STORIES and SONGS

JEWISH BEDTIME STORIES and SONGS

www.**pjlibrary**.org

PJ Library is an international, award-winning program created by the Harold Grinspoon Foundation to support families on their Jewish journeys. To learn more about PJ Library, visit www.pjlibrary.org.

"PJ Library" and "PJ Library Logo" are registered trademarks of the Harold Grinspoon Foundation. All rights reserved.

two lions

Copyright Code: 061415.5K1
ISBN-13: 9781477847947
ISBN-10: 1477847944

The illustrations in this book were created in Corel Painter and Adobe Photoshop.

Book design by Vera Soki
Editor: Margery Cuyler

Printed in China
First edition
10 9 8 7 6 5 4 3 2

Sadie Rose lived on a farm with her mama and papa, four big brothers, one hundred chickens, twenty milk cows, two brown horses, and one barn cat.

Sadie Rose was small and thin and often sickly. Every day, her mama gave her a spoonful of tonic to help her grow, and then Sadie Rose would go collect the chickens' eggs. "I wish I were strong," she told the chickens, but they just squawked and waited for the corn Sadie Rose always brought them.

Across the road from Sadie Rose lived an old woman in a little house. Mrs. Mindel was small and round and often forgetful. Sadie Rose made up a poem to help Mrs. Mindel remember her chores.

"Wipe the table,

sweep the floor,

hang up the apron,

close the oven door."

Sometimes Mrs. Mindel still forgot things, but she would just clop herself on the head and say, "So many holes in this old *kop*!" Then she sang herself songs from the old country.

Every Friday night and every Saturday, Sadie Rose, her family, and their neighbors celebrated the Sabbath at Mrs. Mindel's house. On Friday nights, they sang and prayed and told stories. On Saturdays, they read from the big Torah scroll.

"Our little *shul* in the old country, who could forget it?" the old people would say, remembering their synagogue. "But here, Mrs. Mindel's parlor is our *shul*!"

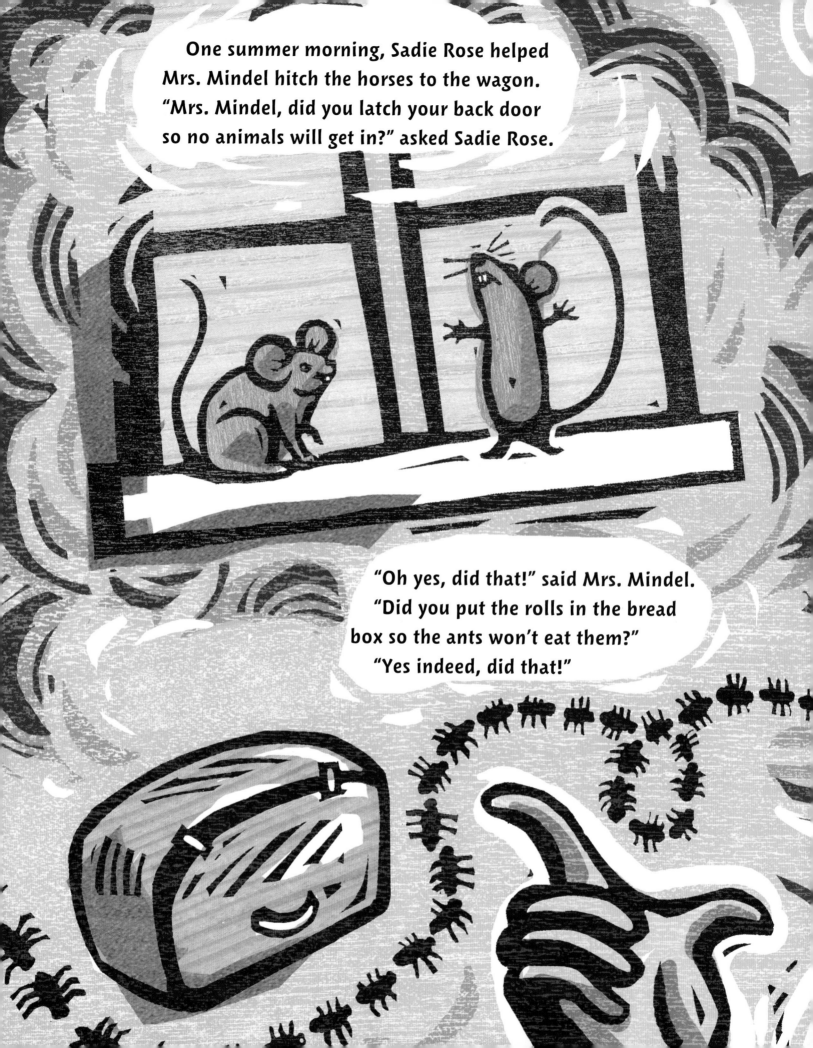

"Did you close the oven door so the coals won't jump out?" Mrs. Mindel scratched her head to help her remember. "The oven door, the oven door," she muttered. "Yes, did that!"

Sadie Rose climbed into the wagon with Mrs. Mindel.

"To town, Bryna! To town, Shayna!" called Sadie Rose. The horses' hooves began to tap on the pebbly road. Soon they reached Sobol's Groceries.

"*Sholom aleichem*," said Mr. Sobol. "What can I get for you today?"

Sadie Rose coughed. Then she said, "Five pounds of flour for the *Shabbos* cakes, one pound of coffee, and twenty short nails to fix the barn door."

"Coming right up," said Mr. Sobol. Then he whispered to Mrs. Mindel, "I'm worried about our Sadie Rose. She's short for six, no? Maybe she's not strong enough for farm life."

Sadie Rose looked up. "I am *eight* years old," she said softly.

"Sam Sobol, I am surprised at you," said Mrs. Mindel loudly. "I thought you knew there's all kinds of strong. Our Sadie Rose, she never forgets a thing. Checks the chicken coops every night so the foxes won't get in. Such a memory that one's got. Give her time; her legs and arms will be strong, too."

Sadie Rose and Mrs. Mindel climbed back into the wagon and drove around the corner to the tailor's shop.

"*Sholom aleichem*," said Mr. Kaufman. "What can I do for you today?"

Sadie Rose coughed. "My papa wants to know if you patched his winter coat," she said.

"Got it all ready for you," answered Mr. Kaufman. Then he whispered to Mrs. Mindel, "I'm worried about our Sadie Rose. Isn't she a little thin for seven? She needs to fatten up, fit in her dress better."

Sadie Rose turned around. "I am *eight* years old," she said clearly.

"Saul Kaufman, I am surprised at you," said Mrs. Mindel. "I thought you knew there's all kinds of strong. Our Sadie Rose, she notices if even the scraggly barn cat's not well. Just last week she took out a stone that got stuck in his paw. Give her time; she'll fill out that dress like she fills up that cat's heart."

Down the block they went to the shoemaker's store.
"*Sholom aleichem*," Mr. Stein said. "What can I do for you?"
Sadie Rose coughed. "We're here to pick up my brother's boots."

Mr. Stein waved two black boots over his head.
"These?" he asked. Sadie Rose nodded.

Then Mr. Stein whispered, "Mrs. Mindel, I'm worried about our Sadie Rose. Coughing, coughing, ever since she was little; and now here she is, six years old and still coughing."

Sadie Rose peered around Mrs. Mindel. "I am *eight* years old," she said firmly.

"Jacob Stein, I am surprised at you," said Mrs. Mindel. "I thought you knew there's all kinds of strong. Our Sadie Rose always comes up with a new idea when you need one. Just yesterday her papa said he needed a milk wagon for his deliveries, but he couldn't figure how to pay for it. So Sadie Rose said, 'Why not buy one with the neighbors and share it?' Give her some time, her lungs will be strong like her mind."

The horses' hooves tapped on the pebbly road out of
town. Close to home, Bryna and Shayna stopped. They
pawed the road and threw back their heads.

Sadie Rose looked down the road toward Mrs. Mindel's
farmhouse. Flames shot from the roof! Smoke swirled
from the windows toward the wagon! Sadie Rose grabbed
Mrs. Mindel's arm.

"The house!" she cried.

"The oven door!" gasped Mrs. Mindel.

Sadie Rose saw her four big brothers throwing buckets of water at the burning house. But as soon as one flame went out, new ones sprang up. Suddenly, her papa raced out the front door clutching the Torah scroll. Just after he reached the path—*crash!* The roof fell in. The porch split in two. Mrs. Mindel's house was gone.

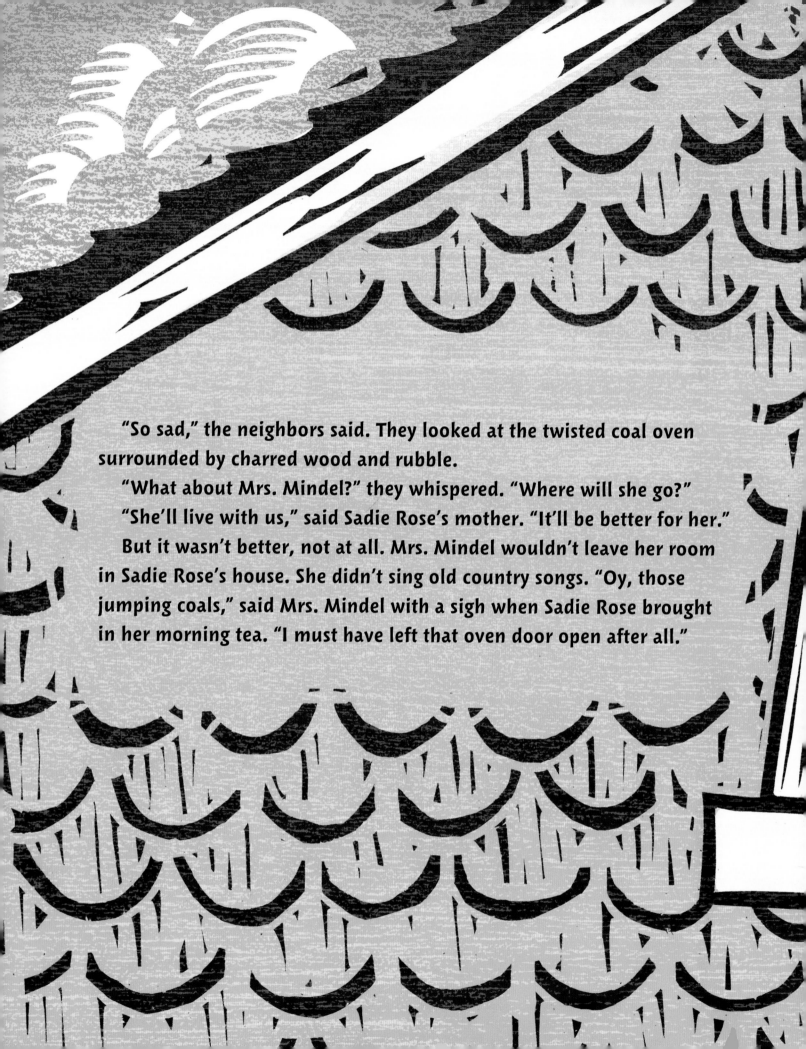

"So sad," the neighbors said. They looked at the twisted coal oven surrounded by charred wood and rubble.

"What about Mrs. Mindel?" they whispered. "Where will she go?"

"She'll live with us," said Sadie Rose's mother. "It'll be better for her."

But it wasn't better, not at all. Mrs. Mindel wouldn't leave her room in Sadie Rose's house. She didn't sing old country songs. "Oy, those jumping coals," said Mrs. Mindel with a sigh when Sadie Rose brought in her morning tea. "I must have left that oven door open after all."

Some Friday nights and Saturdays, Sadie Rose, her family, and their neighbors walked to a farmhouse up the hill for the prayers and Torah reading. Sometimes they walked to a house down the hill. Sometimes they walked to a house through the woods. "Taking turns," said Papa. "It'll be better like this."

But it wasn't better, not at all. The neighbors got confused changing houses and moving the Torah scroll all the time. Some houses weren't big enough for everybody. People pushed. Babies cried. "No good!" said Mrs. Mindel when Sadie Rose told her. "Something must be done."

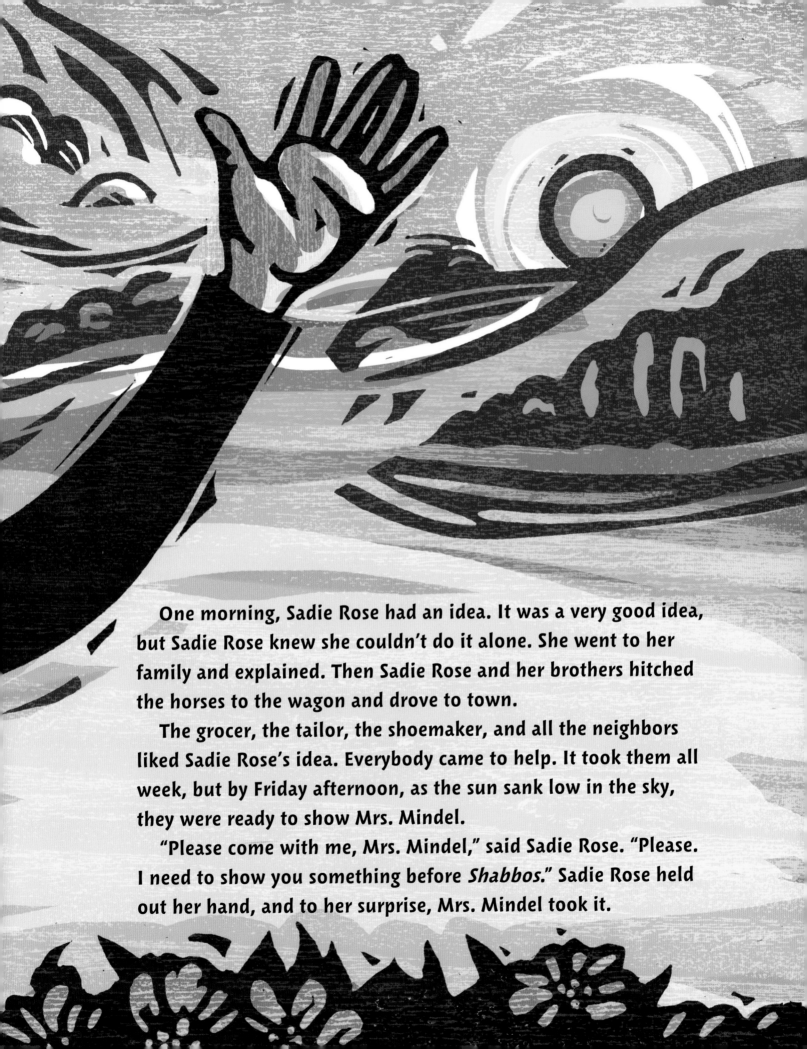

One morning, Sadie Rose had an idea. It was a very good idea, but Sadie Rose knew she couldn't do it alone. She went to her family and explained. Then Sadie Rose and her brothers hitched the horses to the wagon and drove to town.

The grocer, the tailor, the shoemaker, and all the neighbors liked Sadie Rose's idea. Everybody came to help. It took them all week, but by Friday afternoon, as the sun sank low in the sky, they were ready to show Mrs. Mindel.

"Please come with me, Mrs. Mindel," said Sadie Rose. "Please. I need to show you something before *Shabbos*." Sadie Rose held out her hand, and to her surprise, Mrs. Mindel took it.

A small synagogue stood where the farmhouse had been. Through the open door, they could see the Torah scroll, wrapped in a purple cover and resting in a new cabinet. Rows of leather benches waited inside.

"It's for you, Mrs. Mindel," said Sadie Rose.

Mrs. Mindel blinked. Her eyes watered. Then she hugged Sadie Rose.

"No, Sadie Rose!" she cried. "It's for all of us!"

After that, Mrs. Mindel went across the street every day to dust the new *shul*. She straightened the prayer books and shined up the benches. She sang songs from the old country.

And every Friday night and every Saturday morning, Sadie Rose, her family, and their neighbors walked across the road to celebrate the Sabbath at Mrs. Mindel's.

"Our little *shul* in the old country, who could forget it?" the old people would say. "But now we have this beautiful *shul* in our new country!"

"It's Sadie Rose we should thank," called out Sam Sobol.

"Such a girl, our Sadie Rose!" said Mrs. Mindel.

Everyone agreed. Sadie Rose was *all kinds of strong*.

About This Book

During the eleven years I lived in West Hartford, Connecticut, I was lucky to get to know many people who had grown up—or whose parents and grandparents had grown up—on Jewish-owned chicken and dairy farms in the eastern part of the state. I was surprised to learn about these farmers; all the Jewish immigrants I knew had lived in New York or other big cities. Like Mrs. Mindel, these Jewish farmers came from Russia and Eastern Europe (the "old country"). They spoke Yiddish, a colorful language related to German but written in Hebrew characters, and maintained their religious customs, such as *Shabbos* (Sabbath) observance.   —S.R.B.

Glossary

Kop (kohp)—the Yiddish word for head

Shabbos (SHA-bos)—the Yiddish word for the Jewish Sabbath, a day of rest, prayer, singing, storytelling, and delicious foods. *Shabbos* begins at sundown on Friday with the lighting of candles and lasts for twenty-five hours, until three stars appear in the sky on Saturday night. In the present day, both the word *Shabbos* and the Hebrew equivalent *Shabbat* (sha-BAT) are used to refer to the Sabbath.

Sholom aleichem (SHO-lum a-LAYKH-em)—a Yiddish greeting meaning "peace be upon you"

Shul (shool)—Yiddish for *synagogue*, a place for Jewish prayer

Torah (usually pronounced TOE-ruh by English-speaking Jews or toe-RAH by Hebrew speakers; Sadie Rose and her family would have used the Yiddish pronunciation, TOY-ruh)—the Five Books of Moses—the first, and most holy, section of the Hebrew Bible. The Torah tells stories of how the world was created and describes the beginnings of the Jewish people. It also teaches about Jewish laws and some holidays. Each week in synagogue, even today, a different section of the Torah is chanted aloud from a handwritten parchment scroll.